We Have Snow

A CHRISTMAS MIRACLE

ANGELA FRRETT

WE HAVE SNOW: A CHRISTMAS MIRACLE
Copyright © 2022 Angela Errett

This book is a work of fiction. Names, characters, businesses, organizations, places, events, and incidents either are the product of the author's imagination or are used fictitiously. Any resemblance to actual persons, living or dead, events, or locales is entirely coincidental.

For information contact:
Glory Ink, P.O. Box 963, Buckhannon, WV 26201
www.glory-ink.com

Cover and page design by Angelic Designs LLC
Cover Photography by Backyard Photography, Alan Tucker
ISBN: 979-8-9865123-0-3 (paperback), 979-8-9865123-1-0 (ebook)

First Edition: September 2022

10 9 8 7 6 5 4 3 2 1

ACKNOWLEDGEMENTS

This is a prophetic story God gave me to share and offer hope for all those who read it. My prayer is that you enjoy it and receive the hope of Jesus and the coming Kingdom.

THANK YOU

First, thanks to God, with whom all things are possible. Thank you, also, to all my family who have provided a plethora of inspiration over the years. Thank you to my husband for his unique skill of remaining in "stealth mode" while I was writing. A special thank you to my mother, who always inspires me to become a better storyteller, patiently reading every word.

Blessings and Honor,
Angela Errett

1

AUNT MAEVE'S HOUSE

The aroma of pine mixed with cinnamon and the fresh-baked smell of homemade sugar cookies filled the room. Maeve Boulier, seated in front of the oven window, waited for the last batch of sugary delights to come out of the oven. It had been three long years since everyone was last together.

In great anticipation, she finished her pre-Christmas to-do list: pumpkin and sweet potato pies—check, apple streusel—check, cranberry marmalade—check, peanut butter fudge—check, pecan tassies—check, "angeled" eggs—check. And last on her list of things to do before the guests arrived was to bake her famous iced sugar cookies.

She'd sold her first cookie at the neighborhood dime store in the 1950s when she was only thirteen. An outspoken woman entrepreneur, she'd never taken no for an answer and was soon able to get a national food company to buy her recipe, eventually making her CEO of Aunt Maeve's Famous Iced Sugar Cookies. She'd headed up the company while raising her five children in the 1960s with her husband Tom.

The deal was so lucrative—around eight million dollars today—that she willingly added a clause to the contract. Each year, the agreement stated that a designated proxy or Maeve would choose two employees from the Aunt Maeve's Famous Iced Sugar Cookie Corporation and provide them with one-hundred thousand dollars each. She continued to honor her contract by adding more employees along the way. She had been able to bless at least ten employees a year and regularly donated to the local food bank and homeless shelters to boot.

Maeve pushed a strand of her auburn, now slightly silver, hair back from her eyes and peeked again at her cookies. Since that lucrative deal, she'd maintained a strict schedule of rising every day at 5:30 a.m. to read her Bible. She looked across the room to where the old worn book sat next to the table. She came to accept Jesus Christ at the tender age of seven, and throughout her life, she realized if God came first, His goodness prevailed. After her time with God each morning, she walked the path around the property when the weather permitted or exercised on her treadmill in front of the picture window. At least two days a week she'd made it into the office and once a month she presided over the board meetings.

But those outings had stopped this past year. When the pandemic forced her to work from home, Maeve's teleconferencing skills improved, and she even began an online support group for the company. The weekly meetings turned a once dire situation of layoffs and struggles into a mentoring program as she assisted ten of her laid off employees in starting small businesses. She felt good that she'd helped them thrive, despite the lockdowns.

Maeve took the cookies from the oven and transferred them to a rack to cool. While waiting, she iced some others she'd removed from the oven earlier. She'd often made a batch of her famous cookies for Tom in the last year, but now the family was visiting once more like they did before the virus began. This Christmas she'd had to dust off her large batch-making skills for the large quantity of family that would be descending on them soon.

She knew everyone had made their own plans and was elated when all the kids agreed before Thanksgiving to come home this year for Christmas. Even though Tom and Maeve were in their eighties, they were still very active and in good health. Maeve wanted to make sure she got another family Christmas in the books, especially with all the uncertainty the year had thrown at everyone.

Her confirmed dinner guest list of seventy-five included their five children and spouses, seventeen grandchildren, fifteen great-grandchildren, and several friends and business associates. There was surely going to be a couple of stragglers attending as well. Her goal was to gather at least one hundred people to her large two-story Southern ranch house they had built in 2005 in the small community of Zion, West Virginia. Designed with the ever-iconic wraparound porch for socializing, they'd spared no expense to clear and landscape the fifty-acre wooded lot with a large pond to the east. The restoration of the old barn built in the late 1800s offered vast living quarters upstairs for at least twenty guests with a game room and a banquet hall below. With the addition of a large gravel parking area and new horse stables on the south side of the barn, they'd hired three part-time hands and incorporated their side business of horse boarding onto the property.

"Look at the time," Aunt Maeve whispered to herself. "Where has it gone?"

She'd been baking and icing cookies for two hours, and it was now going on 9:30 a.m. To stay on schedule, Maeve needed to finish fast before Sara and Gill arrived.

Her son, Thomas Gillum Boulier Jr.—whom they all called Gill—was the spitting image of his father. Tall with a distinguished square chin, he kept his now graying hair short. Maeve and Tom had been so excited to find out she was pregnant with "Little Gill." In 1960, they had just returned from being stationed in France and were looking for a home in the outskirts of Savannah, Georgia, when Maeve had felt those first baby stirrings.

The nickname "Little Gill" didn't stick after the age of ten, though. That's when Gill took down the schoolyard bully, Timmy Herndon, with one swing. He was coming into his own, and they respected his wish to never be called "Little Gill" again. Still, in Maeve's thoughts, she would always refer to him as her "Little Gill."

WE HAVE SNOW

2

THE WHOLE GANG'S COMING

"Just five more minutes," she thought, "and I'll be done."

She startled when she heard the front screen door snap back to its frame. Gill and Sara had arrived.

"Hey, Mom! I'm home!" Gill shouted. "And

the whole gang's coming!"

Maeve put the last of the icing on the final cookie and placed it in an antique crystal cake saver with a red bow on top as Gill entered the kitchen.

"Oh, Gill, that's great news!" Maeve grinned as she stood for a hug from her oldest son.

"Where's Dad?" Gill inquired.

"He went to mend a five-foot section of the fence line, so Alan and Alana's dog won't get loose," Maeve answered.

Alan and Alana, now six years old, were grandson Zachary's fraternal twins and the youngest great-grandchildren of Tom and Maeve.

"Oh, okay," Gill murmured. "Did you know that Bethany and John won a free trip to Hawaii for Christmas and planned to go next week?"

Bethany was Maeve and Tom's only daughter and Zachary's parents. She shook her head.

"No matter," Gill said a bit to himself. "They changed their plans when they heard the news. They should be here around dark." Before she could question her son about this "news," he continued, "I'm going to get our things. Sara should be right here. I'll go see what's keeping her."

He walked out of the kitchen through the formal dining room toward the side entrance. What "news" was Gill talking about, she wondered as she made her way to arrange the wood in the fireplace for later.

The screen door clacked again and in ran Rufus and the twins, Alan and Alana.

"Hi, Granny!" they yelled in unison as Rufus shook profusely and plopped down on the rug in front of the fireplace.

"Well, hello, children. Thought you wouldn't be here until later today," Maeve replied, giving each of them a quick hug.

"We came with Uncle Jacob and Aunty Mary," Alana explained.

"We begged Mom and Dad, and they finally said yes," Alan added.

Maeve hadn't realized her other son Jacob and his wife Mary had arrived. She tried to look out the front window to the drive, but Alana pulled on her top.

"We wanted to be here early, Granny. It's so exciting!" Alana and Alan grabbed an apple from the fruit bowl sitting on the coffee table and dashed back outside.

Rufus, realizing his pack leaders were on the move, darted toward the door to follow. But missing the open door, he ran right into the screen. A slight yelp came as his momentum stopped abruptly, and his nose poked through.

Maeve couldn't help but giggle as she walked to free the Rhodesian Ridgeback from his embarrassment. She consoled Rufus with a pat on the head and let him out. She felt a warm rush come over her as the sixty-five-degree breeze came across her face. It was so wonderful to have this great weather as the family returned home. The forecast for possible snow on Christmas—now just two days away—would be the icing on her cookie. Tom had asked the stable hands to prepare wreaths for their horses Dancer and Prancer and adorn the winter sleigh with pine, holly, bells, and ribbons just in case there was enough snow.

In the distance, she saw Tom coming back from mending the fence. Fetching him some iced tea, she met him where he stabled his American Painted Horse Lingo.

"Honey," Maeve said as she handed him the glass, "Will you and Gill put some more wood in the wood boxes, please? The weather will be coming in tomorrow night, and I want to make sure we have enough for the house and the barn. And don't forget to check the tie-downs on the decorations. We're supposed to get some high winds as the weather changes. Oh, and maybe you can add fixing the screen door to your to-do list."

"Got you covered." Tom smiled, then took a sip of his tea, accustomed to his wife's lists of demands. "The decorations will withstand a hurricane." He winked. "And I just need to get another load of wood on the front porch. We'll be set for a fortnight, my dear."

"Everyone except Bethany and John will be here shortly after noon, so I've ordered pizza," informed Maeve. "Bethany and John will be here this evening."

"Great!" Tom handed Maeve the now-empty glass and headed for the large woodpile under the lean-to where the four-wheeler and trailer stood waiting.

Maeve laughed as she heard Tom yell, "Hey, Gill. Come help your old man out and let the ladies talk about us!"

"Sure, Dad," Gill replied as he placed the last suitcase on the front porch. His wife Sara came up and gave Maeve a quick hug.

"Hello, Mother." Jacob leaned in to kiss Maeve on the cheek.

"We've missed you," Mary added, and she leaned in for a hug. "So glad we found out in time."

They watched as Alan and Alana played keep-away with Rufus in the driveway, running back and forth, slinging the Frisbee.

"Kids, you may want to head to the field," Jacob prompted. "Don't want you falling in the gravel and hurting yourself."

The twins acknowledged their uncle and merrily skipped toward the field.

"It has been a while since we've all been together, hasn't it?" Maeve said, again wondering when someone would share the "news" Gill had mentioned. And what did Mary mean about "finding out in time?" She brushed the thoughts aside and said, "Your room is ready. Go on up and settle in. I have pizza on the way for lunch, and everyone should be here soon."

WE HAVE SNOW

3

BEFORE SUNDOWN

By three o'clock, the house was teeming with excitement—sons Arthur and Will had arrived with their wives Jane and Cora, kids were running to and fro, empty pizza boxes were strewn across the dining room table, and half-full two-liter bottles of soda sat scattered on the kitchen island.

Some of the older boys and "not so young" boys were in the back yard playing tag football, while Arthur, Will, and Cora did a walking tour of the stables with the younger kids. Mary, along with the older girls sat on the front porch sharing stories and giggling. Jacob, Alan, and Alana were down at the pond trying to catch a fish or two. Rufus was going from one side of the pond to the other, searching for someone to play with him. Finally giving up, he sat beside Alan as the boy threw out his line again and again. Maeve stood at the front door, watching everyone, filled with overwhelming love. What a wonderful sight it was.

Just before sundown, Bethany and John arrived. Alan and Alana ran to greet them and help bring in their bags.

"Mom, we're home!" Bethany yelled as the kids put the bags in the foyer.

Maeve was upstairs and promptly came to greet them.

"Finally, we were getting worried," Maeve said as she hugged Bethany then John. "It's so good to see you both. My heart is now complete. All my kids, their children, and their children's children are home, under one roof again. God is so good to us!"

"Stop it, Mom," uttered Bethany, her eyes filling with tears since it had been so long since her last visit.

Tom came into the living room and swept his daughter up in a big hug. "You better hurry and go wash up. We've got some steaks grilling and all the fixings on the back deck. Just like you like them, John … burnt." Tom slapped his son-in-law on the back and grinned from ear to ear.

"Don't mind him," Maeve said, pulling John into a side hug. "He's been full of himself all afternoon. Maybe we should limit his coffee intake for the next few days. Seems he gets a bit carried away with his jokes when the caffeine kicks in!"

Maeve's heart swelled as everyone laughed. It felt good to see everyone again and have everything right in the Boulier house.

WE HAVE SNOW

4

CHRISTMAS EVE

Maeve woke to the sound of children watching cartoons downstairs and the smell of coffee. She chastised herself for sleeping late. Her plan to keep Tom away from coffee—and cold pizza—would have to wait for another day.

Before she went downstairs, she called over to

the guest house to make sure everyone slept well, letting them know Judy, one of the part-time stable hands and the resident short-order cook, would be preparing breakfast and it would be served in the banquet hall starting around 8:30 a.m.

After Maeve hung up the phone, she wondered again what Gill meant by the "news." No one had said anything more last night. Was there something going on she didn't know about, or was he just talking about everyone coming home? She thought again about Mary saying, "finding out in time." Finding what out in time? It all sounded a bit cryptic, but no matter, the kids were home, and it was Christmas. What more could she want?

Maeve finished getting dressed and went downstairs where Tom greeted her with coffee in her favorite mug.

"Just how you like it dear, two creams, one sugar," Tom said, then kissed her cheek.

"Thanks, honey," Maeve replied. "Are you ready for breakfast?"

"I believe the question is, are *you* ready for breakfast?" he bantered.

Maeve just smiled and said, "Let's go eat."

By now, Gill's strange comment, Mary's odd question, and now Tom's remark intrigued her, but she shrugged it off. Perhaps the family had gotten her something out of the ordinary for Christmas this year.

Judy's scrambled eggs, bacon, sausage, buckwheat pancakes with maple syrup, homemade biscuits, and fresh hash browns delighted everyone for breakfast. As they sat around the table afterward looking stuffed, Maeve waited for some other kind of clue, but no one said anything out of the ordinary.

She filled everyone in on the itinerary for the day—going to town to window shop with the girls, the gun range for those who wanted to practice shooting, or horse riding down to the river. If they didn't feel like being adventurous, they could hang around the always peaceful ranch. The kids, of course, always chose the game room.

Everyone was to meet back up around four o'clock to get ready for dinner at six. Judy was making pork barbecue, curly fries, and green beans, with apple pie, cherry pie crisps, and homemade vanilla ice cream. And, of course, Aunt Maeve's Famous Iced Sugar Cookies.

When the groups convened at the barn earlier than expected, Maeve noticed all the lights were on in the banquet hall and a few extra cars sat in the driveway. But she paid no mind as she stabled her quarter horse Logos and went to the main house to get ready for the dinner.

"Hey, honey," Tom whispered as he sidled up beside her, "Would you mind if we dress up a bit for dinner tonight? It is Christmas Eve. Besides, I like wearing my dress blues any time I can get by with it."

"Sure, if you want to. But remember we're having pork barbecue. You'll want to be careful."

Maeve frowned at his odd request. "What should I wear then? Oh, maybe my green dress with gold trim. Or maybe my white dress with the blue and purple sash. You know … we could pretend like we're back on the Thames River looking at Big Ben and ringing in the New Year."

Suddenly, caught up in the memories of her and Tom's life, she exclaimed, "What a great year that was!"

"Yes, indeed." Tom beamed before saying, "Go with the white dress, honey. You look so lovely in it."

"White dress it is," Maeve agreed. "But I'll need a bib!" They both snickered and continued getting ready.

5

THE CALM BEFORE THE STORM

The house was eerily quiet a few minutes before six as Maeve glided down the stairs to meet Tom at the front door.

"Wow!" Tom's eyes grew wide when he caught sight of her, then pulled her close. He kissed Maeve on the hand, obviously stunned by her appearance. "Honey, you are just as beautiful as the day I married you."

"Oh, Tom, you spoil me." Maeve felt her cheeks grow warm. "Where is everyone? Are they all over at the barn?"

"Yes." Tom pulled her hand through the crook of his elbow. "All ready and waiting for us."

"Well, this family never ceases to amaze me," she said as she let Tom lead her out the door.

"True. Don't think I have ever witnessed them all being able to be on time"—He paused to ponder—"Ever!" Turning back to Maeve, he asked, "You ready?"

"Ready as I'll ever be, my Marine," Maeve proclaimed.

As they left the front porch, Maeve noticed the wind had picked up and the temperature had dropped. She snuggled closer to Tom and focused on the barn once more. Something was different. The barn had more lights on, and no one was lingering outside. Were they already all in the barn? Even Rufus?

They continued their walk, holding tight to one another without saying a word. Maeve felt Tom shiver and wondered if he was feeling a chill as they approached the double barn doors. She felt herself getting a little weak in the knees and hoped it was because of the night's excitement and not her blood sugar dropping.

Instead of opening the doors, Tom knocked, and they began to open.

Before Maeve could ask what he was doing, she glimpsed the glorious sight before her. Soft white lights hung everywhere in-between panels of white linen banners. The tables were adorned with crystal drinkware and gold plates with enormous white and red flower arrangements and white candles. Strings of crystals had been draped from the rafters, and the light reflected rainbows across the white linen tablecloths. Around each table, chairs covered in white with large bows and red roses in the back awaited their guests. The buffet table was decorated in the same flowers and candles, but there was an area to the right with a large white curtain hanging from the ceiling, just at the edge of the parquet dance floor. A small string ensemble was playing classical music beside it.

As Tom and Maeve entered, everyone clapped and cheered. Maeve felt like a princess, and Tom was her knight in shining armor. Maeve then realized everyone was dressed in white except Tom. Then she noticed two large gold-toned chairs and a table in the front facing the other tables.

"Oh my, Tom," she said, perplexed, "What is all this?"

"Honey, you always do everything you can for everyone." Tom turned to her and said, "so this year for Christmas, we want you to have everything done for you."

"This is overwhelming," Maeve whispered.

"Just enjoy, my dear," Tom whispered against her ear.

"Say the prayer over the food, Dad, so we can get this feast underway," Arthur yelled.

"Yay, Dad, let's roll," William added as everyone snickered.

"Okay, okay," Tom answered. He led Maeve to her seat which he pulled out for her to sit. Then he began his prayer.

"Dear Heavenly Father, we come before You on this beautiful night and ask that Your Spirit be with us. We ask for strength from our food, Your Word for our spirit, and this meal for our bodies, and that no part shall bring us harm. We seek Your wisdom and thank You for Your Son, Jesus, who died to give us life more abundantly. We thank You for the anointing of Christ and the grace and mercy offered for all those who believe. In Jesus's name, we pray, amen."

Dinner turned out to be a five-course catered meal, not barbecue, from a local chef who was the son of one of Tom's buddies in the Marines. Everyone went back for seconds, and the tiramisu was exquisite. There was no way this Christmas was going to get any better than it was at this very moment, Maeve thought.

Then, at the table in the far-right corner, a man stood and clanged his spoon against his water glass.

"Everyone! Listen up!" he yelled.

Maeve knew that voice. Pastor Mitchell.

The ensemble halted their rendition of Felix Mendelssohn's Octet, and the hall grew silent.

"This Christmas Eve," Pastor Mitchell began,

"we have had the pleasure of being in the presence of one of the most loving, caring, most beautiful souls ever placed on this earth, Mrs. Maeve Boulier. Better known as Aunt Maeve."

Everyone began to clap.

"Maeve is one who even keeps the pastor in line," Pastor Mitchell continued.

Laughter filled the room, and people shook their heads in agreement.

"Now, that is not a bad thing," he exclaimed, "I just wish I realized I was wrong before she got a hold of me!"

The crowd rolled with laughter again.

Clang, clang, clang went the spoon on the glass once more, and the crowd hushed again.

"But seriously folks, Maeve is a seeker of the Kingdom, and God is with her. I could go on with so many stories, but I want to remain faithful to what this evening is about. It's about being with friends and family. It's about breaking bread with those you love and who love you. It's about the Spirit of God that brings so much love and peace during the holiday season. And we know that you must receive the Gospel of Jesus Christ, believe it, and be filled with the Holy Spirit.

"But tonight, is even more special than Maeve knows. I was contacted by Gill, who was the main coordinator of this night, by the way."

Applause filled the room again.

The pastor held up his hands again for quiet. "I was contacted by Gill," Pastor Mitchell continued, "who said he had been speaking with the family about what would mean the most to Maeve. Each of them told me their mom would like her whole family to enter the Kingdom of God.

"Now, some of you all, and you know who you are"—he paused to look around the room which was followed by the giggling of the crowd—"have been sitting on the fence. While others broke the fence down and stepped on it."

Laughter ejected, once more.

"I personally spoke to each of the family members, and tonight is a declaration of what each of them has agreed to. Each agrees that being in God's family trumps any other thing they could ever hope or do on this earth.

"So, with each person's declaration of faith confirmed by me, I would like to call those who agreed to be baptized tonight up, and we will get the real party started!"

Thunderous applause echoed across the hall as all those family members who had not yet been baptized stepped forward, and the large white curtain was dropped to reveal a baptismal.

Maeve gasped. She could not believe her eyes. All those mornings, sitting in the breakfast nook, praying not only for the salvation of her family but for their entrance into the Kingdom of God, was happening tonight, on Christmas Eve. A glorious event that could only be orchestrated by God!

One after another, Jacob, Mary, Bethany, John, and the twins, Alan and Alana—twenty-four in all—declared Jesus as Lord. Each one came to Tom and Maeve and hugged them before entering the baptismal. And, as you can imagine, there was not a dry eye in the house.

WE HAVE SNOW

6

CHRISTMAS MORNING

Maeve could hardly sleep that night, forcing herself to stay in bed until her usual 5:30 a.m. alarm the next morning. When it finally went off, she slipped downstairs to turn on the tree, start the coffee, and light the fireplace. The great room was decked out in gold and silver, and the twenty-foot tree with all white lights was almost dwarfed by the number of gifts around it. How the kids were able to sneak all those gifts in without waking everyone was a miracle.

Tom rustled up a piece of leftover pizza and joined Maeve in the great room.

"Well, dear, did you get everything you wanted for Christmas?" Tom asked, sitting down next to her, and gazing at the tree.

"Tom, I have a few more trips around the sun, Lord willing," Maeve offered up, "but I have to admit, there will never be another Christmas like this."

They sat in silence on the love seat, watching the flames and holding each other.

"Hey, did you look outside yet?" grinned Tom.

"And just like that, the icing on the cookie," Maeve answered, "we have snow."

Thanks for reading *We Have Snow: A Christmas Miracle.* Please add a short review on Amazon and let me know what you thought!

Visit www.glorymagazinewv.com and join our email list. Receive new issue notifications and read prophetic articles with insight into Kingdom living.

ABOUT THE AUTHOR

Angela Errett founded Angelic Designs LLC in 2005 and in 2013 became founder and writer for *Glory Magazine*, an online Christian magazine. She loves spending time with the Lord, her husband, the great outdoors, and her family. She is committed to bringing forth stories from Christian authors through her new publishing venture, Glory Ink. To find out more about Angela, visit www.angelicdesigns.com/about-us.

"I will stand upon my watch, and set me upon the tower, and will watch to see what he will say unto me, and what I shall answer when I am reproved. And the Lord answered me, and said, Write the vision, and make it plain upon tables, that he may run that readeth it."

Habakkuk 2:1-2 KJV

www.ingramcontent.com/pod-product-compliance
Lightning Source LLC
Chambersburg PA
CBHW060509300726
48975CB00008B/2714